Warning
This book contains bad words like-
butt, bum, fart, honkers, dork, bottom and more.
It also contains references to awesome computer games,
boys picking on girls, girls picking on boys,
and very mild bad behaviour.
If you don't wish your child to be exposed to this nonsense,
then don't get this book
BUT
They will miss out on a great story, funny jokes, lots of laughs,
whacky illustrations, how to deal with bullies,
a lovely moral message,
and seeing boys and girls getting along very nicely.
And they will be READING!!!
WARNING

D1112923

OTHER BOOKS BY KATE CULLEN

Available on Amazon as eBooks or print books

Game on Boys 2 : Minecraft Madness (8-12)

Game on Boys 3 : No Girls allowed (8-12)

Diary Of a Wickedly Cool Witch : Bullies and Baddies (10-13)

Lucy the Easter Dog (Early readers Ebook)

Lucy goes to the Halloween Party (Early readers Ebook)

Lucy the Christmas Dog (coming soon)

Game on Boys 4 (coming soon)

Connect with KATE on

gameonboysseries@gmail.com or follow at

Kate Cullen at katekate5555

Written and Illustrated by Kate Cullen

ISBN 978 1500631932

Game On Boys!

The PlayStation Playoffs

Written and Illustrated
By Kate Cullen

Dedication

This is for all the kids who can't get enough of their computer games, and for all the parents who can't get their kids to read enough books because of computer games, and for all the teachers out there who do an amazing job teaching kids to read in the first place. ☺

Contents

Chapter 1: Bottoms at school

I'm going to tell you something really weird. I mean super weird. You're going to think I'm really stupid. In fact you'll probably think I'm a real dork. My sister does and I know because she's always telling me. The truth is, I *love* going to school. No I'm not kidding, if that's what you just thought to yourself.

My name is Ryan, and I go to the greatest school in the whole world *and* I have the best teacher in the whole school. Mr Higginbottom is his name. That's right Higgin BOTTOM. Can you believe it? When he walked into the classroom on the first day of term, he wrote it on the blackboard and said, "Ok everyone, that's right, my name is Bottom, Higginbottom to be precise. Lets all get it over with, say it out loud and then we can have a big laugh. BOTTOM, BOTTOM, BOTTOM. Come on everybody, lets shout it out."

We all burst into laughter and from that day on he has been the coolest teacher ever. It's a pity about his name though, but he lets us call him Mr H so it's not so embarrassing.

Mr Higginbottom rocks

Good grades
+
Good Behavior
= Computer Games
77+
32
83+
65
Best Teacher

My big sister thinks I'm weird because I love going to school so much. She doesn't understand though, because she's just a stinky girl who's always glued to her phone and making things with rubber bands. I call them Doom bands. What do girls know anyway? All they ever think about is cutesy, pukey makeup and revoltingly bizarre dolls that go to monster schools. Batz dolls I call them, with their oversized heads, puffy lips and only half a leg. Lisa is twelve going on eighteen, well she thinks she is anyway, the way she dresses. I guess she is kind of pretty, in a fake sort of way. Just ask her, she'll tell you how gooooorgeous she is.

My Mom thinks it's wonderful that I love school and she's forever skiting (that means bragging) to her friends how well I do. She says she can't believe the change in me because I used to hate school in first grade. I still remember screaming like a fire engine with tears rolling down my face and snot pouring out of my nose clinging onto her chubby legs as she tried to leave. Yuk! I can't believe I used to be such a baby. How embarrassing is that?

But now that I'm in fifth grade, there's no way I would miss a day of school. Uh uh, NO WAY! And there's no way I would let snot pour out of my nose either. To miss a day at school would put at risk going to one of *the* best places on Earth. Well… maybe it's not *the* best place. Zone Ten might be a little bit better. And this one time when we went on holidays to visit my Pop, I went to another place called Football Hero world. All the games were interactive and linked up to gigantic computer screens. You even got to see yourself being a TV presenter on a footy show on TV. It was awesome. Dad said I did a better job than Al Michaels and Emmet Smith put together, and Mom said I was better looking than Tom Brady. I don't know what they were going on about but it was a pretty cool place.

Actually, it could even be better than Zone Ten. But I probably won't get to go again as Pop died and went to this other cool place called heaven where our dog lives.

Our dog Pugsley went to heaven because he got bitten by a green ant and died. Mom said he just got old and sick but Dad reckons he was riddled with green ant bites from rolling on the front lawn and they sucked the life out of him. Now he's always telling me not to wrestle my neighbor Fletch on the grass in case we get bitten by green ants as well. I think he's probably telling one of those white lies that only adults are allowed to tell to stop me doing kung fu on the front lawn with Fletch. Sometimes we do get a bit rough I guess.

The other day I accidently kicked him in the nuts and he went home squealing like a girl. It was just an accident. In case Dad is telling the truth about Pugsley and the green ants I always wear shoes now when I wrestle Fletch on the grass. That's probably why it hurt him so much. Better than being bitten by a green ant though.

Now I have this obsession with green ants. The other day when I was eating my tea I had a weird thought about them. I asked Mom what it would be like if a green ant went into the bread roll that I was eating. We were having homemade Macca's hamburgers which Mom says are exactly the same as Macca's burgers except she makes them at home with love. They're much yummier though 'cos they don't have the green thing in the middle. I've never worked out why the people at McDonalds put the green thing in because everyone always throws it out. Even my Dad takes it out of his, and he has three burgers!

Mom never eats fast food because she's always starting a diet. Plus she says it's not good for you and doesn't taste very nice. What would she know anyway? She thinks cauliflower and broccoli taste nice. But I know she always manages to sneak a few bites of every-ones else's burgers when she thinks we're not watching. Dad rolls his eyes and says "Why don't you get your own?"
"Because it teaches everyone how to share," Mom always replies. Mom works at the hospital as a food technician in the kitchen three days a week which I think means making the grub and dishing it out. It makes her a bit obsessed about food though I think. The other four days she says she works as a shopping technician but she doesn't get any money for that. Dad reckons

on those days she just spends all the money she makes on the other three days.

So, as I was munching on a bit of crispy, green lettuce the other day, I had this really interesting thought at the dinner table about green ants.
"Mom, what would happen if the green ant crawled into the roll and got lost in the forest of lettuce and then I ate it and it travelled all the way down to my heart and bit it? Would it really hurt?"

She paused with a blank look on her face. "No probably not, because I don't think the heart would feel it."

"Would I die?"

"No I don't think so."

"Would it cause me to have a heart attack?"

"No I don't think so." Why do adults sometimes pretend they know the answer when they really don't, but they disguise the fact by saying, "I think so or I don't think so?"

Mr Higginbottom would have known the answer to that. He knows just about everything because he's the best teacher in the whole wide world. That brings me to the reason of why I go to the very best school around and why I love school so much. I know you'll probably think I'm really weird but believe me, I'm not. If you got to do what I do at my school you'd be on ya skateboard and coming to my school before you could say "*Higginbottom rules!*"

Chapter 2: Paper, Chocolate and Buckets

It's because of Mr H and this really exciting thing that he lets us do that makes me love going to school so much. Every afternoon at a quarter to three, Mr Higginbottom gets out his big, black book and looks at all the names of the kids in my class and checks who has been really good and who has completed all the work for the day. Then he always makes a big announcement in a really silly voice.

"Ok kiddie widdies, grade fivey wiveys." And then he quickly changes his tone to a commander in the army style. "The Criteria for the day is as follows. ……

Number 1. You must have completed page 33 in your Maths book.

Number 2. You must have copied down all of the work from the whiteboard.

Number 3. You must have received twenty out of twenty for your spelling this morning, and last, but certainly not least, the final criteria for the day is, you must not have been spoken to by me, or any of the other wonderful human beings that inhabit this Earth, better known as teachers, for getting into trouble at all anytime today."

He would always make sure there was one thing on the list that we didn't know whether we'd achieved or not just to be tricky. Then he would take a big breath at the end as though he were gasping for life. It was always so exciting to wait and hear whether your name would be called out or not.

"And so," he would continue, "the students who have achieved all the criteria for today are as follows…………"

Sometimes there were lots of kids on the list and sometimes there were only a few. I was *always* on the list. There was no way I would ever risk not getting on the list so I always made sure I did all my work on time. Sometimes my friend Matthew would try and make me shoot spit balls at the girl's heads, but I try my hardest to ignore him. Gee it's hard though, because it's really funny when the spit balls whack them on their ear or neck and they think it's a mosi biting them. They start flapping their arms around their head at nothing, looking like idiots, not realising we are cacking ourselves laughing behind their backs.

I don't dare do it now though. If Mr Higginbottom saw me, it would be instant disqualification because he always has the same criteria (rules) that no-one is allowed to get into trouble or be told off during the day. Everybody that meets the criteria gets their name called out and gets to choose from his big green bucket. You can either choose a chocolate bar or a raffle ticket. A chockie bar is yummy, but a raffle ticket is just plain awesome, *and* a gateway to gamers Heaven. If you choose a raffle ticket it goes into the red bucket for the big draw before lunch on Friday.
The eight kids with the most raffle tickets on Friday get to do something really sick during Friday lunch time *and* all afternoon during class time in the computer room. It's so unreal. Sometimes I can't believe how cool it is. I have to pinch myself to make sure I'm not dreaming.

Chapter 3: The Great Computer Room

The computer room is between our classroom and Miss Egbutt's classroom and no-one is allowed to enter without permission or without a teacher. It's full of computers, televisions, DVD's, cd players and all sorts of other high tech electronics. In the far corner of the room, there's a huge book shelf that has a lot of DVD's and computer games all arranged in alphabetical order.

There's nothing very exciting though, mostly just boring games that you can learn stuff from like 'The Maths Magician' and 'The Spelling Sorcerer'. I once had a sneaky look in the B section for Batman, under S for Spiderman and under T for the Teenage Mutant Ninja Turtles, but there was nothing. Zilch. Zip. Zippo. They didn't even have any of the Avengers stuff and that's the first letter of the alphabet.

Mom says it's probably because they're rated M and are full of violence with no educational value. What would she know? All the boys I know in Fifth grade have been to see The Dark Knight at the movies and they haven't suffered mentally from the experience or turned into raging criminals jailed at ten.

The coolest part though, is when Mr Higginbottom gets out his big black brief case and pulls out, not one, not two, but three PlayStation 3 consoles. It's so exciting. My Mom says I'm obsessed with PlayStation (and Minecraft) but what would she know? She doesn't even know what a memory card is. She probably thinks a memory card is something you slot into your brain to help you remember things.

Inside his big black case is every PS3 game you can imagine; Fifa, Star Wars, Need for Speed, NBA and Skylanders. Of course he's not allowed to bring any that are above a pg rating. He says we have to respect our parents and the rules of the school. Once we begged and begged him to bring Grand Theft Auto but he said that it would jeopardise the chance to play PS3 at school. I didn't really know what that meant. Sometimes he uses really big words just to confuse us I think. So I asked Mom what jeopardised meant and she said "Look it up in the dictionary". She *always* does that to me.

"But Mom, can't you just tell me so it's quicker?"

"Well why don't I just sit down and do all your homework for you too?"

"Ok," I replied. "That's a good idea." I thought Mom was being nice for a change but she was just being sarcastic. In the end she helped me look it up, and it meant that if you jeopardise something, you put it in a position where you might lose it, or it might be in danger. Well we definitely didn't want to jeopardise our chance to play PS at school by bugging Mr H to bring in Grand Theft Auto.

Chapter 4: A Pee in a Cup

Every Friday, the eight of us that make the cut go into the computer room at lunchtime and it's so exciting. We get to choose what game we want to play and who we want to verse. Sometimes even Mr H plays with us. It's so cool if you get to verse him 'cos he's an awesome player. He reckons he's even got a PlayStation 4 and an X box at home and that one day he might bring them in. Wow! That would be so cool man.

Last Friday morning he played a really funny trick on me. I thought for a moment that I wasn't going to make it into the club that day by not getting all my spelling words right. At the time I couldn't see the humor in it, but now I think about it, I guess it was sort of funny.

"Right, grade fivey wivies, the last lesson before lunch is a super spelling bee. Everyone gets one word and they need to get it right," he said. Yuk! I hate spelling. Mom always makes me do these sight words before I'm allowed to go outside and wrestle Fletch, my next door neighbor.

When it came to my turn in the super spelling bee everyone had already been given really easy words. "Ryan," Mr H said, "I want you to spell the word icup."

"Icup?" I thought. I clammed up and my face went all warm and prickly; that feeling you get when you know you're going to get the answer wrong. It's a bit like the feeling you get when you walk up on stage to collect an award and you trip going up the stairs in front of everyone, or worse still, your pants fall down. It's called embarrassment and I was feeling it big time.

Actually it was worse than big time. It was humongous, mammoth, big time. All those long, boring afternoons sitting with Mom on the couch spelling word after word meant nothing anymore. I'd never heard of the word 'icup'. "Oh no," I thought. If I got this wrong I might not make the necessary criteria to get a raffle ticket before the big draw. Panic stations set in. This was going to be disastrous.

Mom always said that if you get nervous or frightened, just imagine everyone around you is only in their underwear. It will make you laugh and you'll forget your nerves. So I did, but it wasn't a pretty sight.

"Ok get a grip of yourself Rino," I said in my head. "Think about it and just sound the word out." I could hear my Mom's words bleating in my head as she so often did when I got stuck on a word. I began slowly, deep in thought and not willing to put one foot wrong sounding out each letter, "I … c.. u .. pee." There was silence and then the whole class erupted into hysterics, laughing their heads off, followed by Mr Higginbottom. Then I realised what I had just said when I sounded out the word; "I see you pee," and I burst out into an embarrassed sort of laughter too.

Mr Higginbottom came over and gave me a friendly pat on my head and ruffled my hair. It didn't worry me that I'd combed it just the right way and put jell in it that morning. It was ok for Mr H to mess it up but if my sister ever did it, she'd be dead meat.

"Well done," he said. "I knew you would be cool enough to take a harmless joke. It's a bit of a silly joke," he told the rest of the class. "But silly jokes are ok if you just don’t let them go too far. You can have a free raffle ticket for your trouble.”

“I know another one like that,” said Mitch who was the class clown. “Spell pig backwards,” he shouted out before Mr H got a chance to say anything. Mr H scratched his head and looked down. “Ok, ok what have I started here?” he mumbled. “I think we’ll finish up with the silly jokes now Mitch and get down to serious business and do the proper spelling test.”

As soon as the test was over and marked, Mr H sat himself down on the mat with his legs crossed like he was in kindergarten. "Now my little munchkins, it's time to announce the names of the people who will be selecting a delectable chocolate or a scrappy bit of paper out of my beautiful green bucket here." He always said such silly things.

"Ok," he said, "there are only six students that made all the criteria today because of this morning's pea shooting incident. Matthew Robinson and Kevin Cameron, you both scored top marks today for all your work…"

"Yeahh!" Matthew and Kevin both shouted with excitement at the sound of their names being called out.

"Hang on, hang on," said the teacher getting a bit annoyed at them for yelling out. "If you would please refrain from calling out and let me finish before you get too excited. Now, as I was saying before your little vocal explosion, you scored very well the whole week but…. because you were both involved today flicking rubber bands and making weapons out of scrunched up bits of paper and pens, which got you into trouble, you unfortunately do not satisfy all the criteria to warrant a raffle ticket or a chocolate bar today. Sorry boys, you know that's one of the golden rules of the game."

Matthew and Kevin both looked pretty sad and sulky. I thought Matthew was going to cry. He's one of my best mates and he's heaps of fun but sometimes he just gets into trouble a bit too much. When we get into the PlayStation club together we like to verse each other but he doesn't always get in because he mucks around in class more than he should.

The other week he missed out because he was caught making fart sounds with his arms in the classroom with Pete and Jay. Mr H went into the office next door for five minutes to do something important or so he said. It was probably to blow Miss Egbutt a kiss. He said we all had to do silent reading which is pretty impossible since half the grade are still reading picture books out loud. Everyone was quiet and all of a sudden there was a fart sound. There were a few quiet sniggers followed by another fart sound and more laughs. It was a real honker. When I turned around I could see them making the noises by putting their fists under their arms and squashing them. It's heaps fun to do. We do it all the time in the play ground but there was no way I was going to risk popping off in the classroom.

Even though I like Matthew heaps, sometimes I think that when God was handing out brains, Matthew must have been mucking around and missed out. He was probably making fart sounds in his Mommy's tummy somewhere.

Sitting way down in the back corner laughing hysterically at their repulsive sound making, their eyes gleaming with pride, they didn't notice our teacher hovering behind the office door capturing the whole scene in front of him. As he stepped calmly into the room he spoke with a quietly calm tone. "Matthew, Jay, Peter! In my office, *now*!" Matthew knew right at that ghastly moment he probably wouldn't get a raffle ticket that day. Instead he spent half the day outside the headmaster's office.

So he was extra sad when he found out he would have to miss out again because of silly behavior two weeks in a row. But as my Mom says, he can choose to be silly or he can choose to be sensible. My Mom thinks she knows everything. Dad says she's wise and he's always saying, "Listen to your Mother," even though *he* never does.

Now the other criteria for this particular day was that homework had to be handed in, all maths sheets completed with at least 80 percent correct, all spelling words correct and one book report completed. I was pretty confident that I would be getting a raffle ticket because I'd done everything on the list and was certain all my maths was correct because Mom checked it and *I* definitely hadn't got into trouble all week. But one could never be too certain.

Chapter 5: Where was my Name?

Mr Higginbottom continued, "So the lucky people for today are….." He paused, "and at this moment I would like to point out that I have some scrumptiously delicious chocolate bars here today bigger than usual." Now if there's anyone that loves chocolate it's me. I love chocolate more than anything, except… PlayStation and Minecraft, so there was no way I was going to choose a measly chocolate bar no matter how big it was, over a possible whole afternoon in the computer room.

He continued, "And so the winners are… Sophie Delaney, Grace Mitchell, Craig Williams…" Sophie squealed like my big sister does. Girls are so annoying the way they squeal and giggle and stuff. They're so… girlie! Everyone knew she would be going for the biggest block of chocolate. Sophie was fat but we weren't allowed to tease her because teasing is cruel and as my Mom would always say, "Just because she's a bit on the podgy side doesn't mean she's not a lovely, intelligent girl."

Grace and Craig chose chocolate bars as well of course. Craig is too sissy to choose a raffle ticket and maybe get a go in the club. Grace chose a crunch bar which is my favourite but I didn't care. I didn't want chocolate. I was happy with just a raffle ticket. Anyway my Mom reckons chocolate's not good for you. What would she know though? She says brussels sprouts and broccoli are good for you. Yuk! That's puke food. Anything that tastes like spew can't be good for you. I think she just pretends chocolate is bad for you so she can have it all to herself. Sometimes when I'm sneaking around the top shelf in the pantry when Mom's not watching I see a block of chocolate and the next morning, it's gone. She says it must be the tooth fairies getting rid of it. As if!

"And the last people that make all the necessary criteria today are," Mr Higginbottom continued, "are Jacob, Nigel and let's see, who might the lucky last person be...? Ellie Sanders." My heart sank when I didn't hear my name called out. It felt like it was doing a triple somersault then spiralling downwards into a quick bungee jump onto the ground smashing into billions of pieces. Where was my name? *Where was my name*?

Chapter 6: Reality Checks in

What happened to my name? I didn't know whether to put up my hand and risk embarrassment or suffer in a sulky silence and pretend I didn't care. What if I had got all the maths sums wrong? Everyone would know. I was in a dilemma. It was way too risky. If I didn't get a raffle ticket I might not have enough to be in the top eight. Mr H had even said that he had a really special announcement to make to the PS gang. That's what we called the boys who always got to play in the computer room.

Nigel Roberts walked passed me on his way to collect a raffle ticket. He'd had one every day and was sure to get in the top eight. He gave me a bit of a spiteful smirk and bumped into my arm as he walked passed. "Bad luck Rino, you missed out," and then under his breath he said, "suckerrrrr!" Nigel's the type of guy who likes to be mean. His dark, cropped hair and his big heavy rimmed glasses make him look a bit nerdish but he's actually pretty smart. He just doesn't know how to be nice. In fact it's probably the only word in the English language that he can't spell. Some kids are just like that.

I felt that warm, squishy feeling at the back of my eyes, the one you get right before you start to cry. If my big sister was there, she would have made fun of me and called me a cry baby. I couldn't do it. I had to stop my self. There had to be a logical explanation for my name not being on his list. It had to be a mistake. Even Mr H was allowed to make a mistake. He was only human after all. Maths wasn't my best subject but there was no way I wouldn't have got at *least* eighty percent.

As the class went back to their normal business of trying to learn stuff while thinking about lunch break I slowly put up my hand.

"Yes Ryan," Mr Higginbottom said from his desk in a loud voice that attracted most of the kid's attention.

"Could you come here please Mr Higginbottom?" I asked sheepishly. I really didn't want to question his decision out loud. He came over. I looked around to make sure no one was listening.

"Um," I hesitated for a moment and breathed deeply. "I was just wondering how come I didn't get all the criteria to get a raffle ticket today."

"H'mm, let's see, it *is* a bit unlike you not to accomplish everything." He grabbed his clipboard from the desk and came back. "Ok let's see. You got ten out of ten for spelling this morning, very good. And you got eight out of ten for the maths sheet. That's pretty good stuff too, exactly eighty percent." I was trying to peak over his shoulder to see if there were any big red crosses. "You haven't been in trouble today. In fact I don't think you've been in trouble all year. You completed the book report, ahh, here we go, you didn't hand in your homework this morning." He looked up at me with his bushy eyebrows frowning as they descended down to the bridge of his nose.

"Ryan, that's not like you at all."

'Of course it's not like me,' I thought. 'It's not me! It's not me, because I *did* hand it in'.

"But sir, I did hand it in. I put it in the box. I'm sure I did." My heart was starting to beat faster. Was my memory failing me or had my stupid, rotten sister played a trick on me again like she did at the start of the year when she took my homework out after Mom had packed it in my bag?

She's the sort of sister who does that. She's also the sort of sister who takes all your jocks from your bag before you go on camp! She's the sort of sister who puts prawns in your school bag even on a hot day. Yes! She did that too. Once I even found dog poo in my shoe though she swears that wasn't her. Did she think I would blame Pugsley for mistaking my shoe for a toilet seat?

Now I was sure I remembered putting my homework in the box that morning or was that the day before? Now I was beginning to doubt myself. How could I put up a convincing argument if I couldn't even believe myself? I was turning into a droll troll who had no idea what they were talking about.

"Hang on let me have a double check in the box," said Mr H coming to my rescue. I think he sensed that my eyes were getting that wet, soggy feeling happening behind my bulging sockets again. The last thing he would want to do would be to console a blubbering and emotional ten year old boy. My Mom always says I get too emotional over the PlayStation. What does she know? I don't even know what getting emotional means. She just says it means getting upset and crying a lot. My sister says it means cracking it all the time.

"No there's nothing here. Have you checked your bag? Go and have another look. If you can find it now I'll give you a second chance." I quickly looked in my bag but there was nothing. Again I felt despair and desperation as if my heart was coming in for another sky dive southwards at the speed of super sonic radar. This could not be happening. Reality was checking in. I was *not* going to be sitting in the computer room that afternoon if I didn't get that ticket.

Chapter 7: The Case of the Missing Homework

I could feel a bit of the squishy warm fluid begin to escape from the corner of my eye. Forget my sister calling me a cry baby, the whole class who had started to take notice of the grand trial would soon know me as 'the big, sooky bubba'. I was a big baby who couldn't hold back tears.

"Hang on a minute, what's this down the back of my desk?" Mr H's words rang out like Santa Claus' sleigh bells ringing in my ears as I quickly pushed the escaping tear back into its socket where it safely belonged undetected.

"Aha!" he said. "This looks like one homework book in the name of Master Ryan James." His eyebrows left his nose and stretched up to his fringe as his expression changed to amusement.

"So, the million dollar question is.... is there a hole in my box big enough to let this quite large book slip through or has someone been a little careless in putting the homework into the inside of the box?" His eyebrows dashed between his nose and fringe blinking at me in a light accusatory way.

I remembered back to that morning when Matthew and I raced to see who could get on the mat first. In my rush to get there first, I made a quick detour to throw the homework in the box and slid into landing at the front of the mat as I yelled, "*INCOMING*". Mr H was still outside waiting for some of the latecomers to arrive otherwise I wouldn't have done it.

Anyway, I won. I got to the mat first but it was now clear to me that in my rush, somehow the home work book had not met successfully with its intended destination. Luckily for me the case of the missing book had been solved and was now safely in the hands of the master.

I could sense the sweet smell of victory once again. I looked at my teacher with the nicest, sweetest smile I could summons. I reminded myself of the dim-witted girls in the class whenever he asked who wanted to do a job for him. All the sucky girls would always sit up straighter than a light pole and smile sweetly like they had fairy floss dripping out of their mouths and fluorescent signs on their head saying 'pick me, pick me'. They would wait in pathetic anticipation for him to choose them and when he didn't, they would go back to their sloppy postures and sulky faces until the next time.

"Well class shall I give him a second chance and give him a raffle ticket today?" Half the class yelled out yes and some of the others who liked to hang it on every body said no just to be annoying pains. I knew Mr Higginbottom would let me. He was such a cool teacher.

"Well you must have caught me at a soft moment. Ok then Ryan, come and collect your prize." He patted me on the back in a friendly way as I raced up to the green bucket. "I wonder what Master Ryan is going to collect," he teased. "Will it be this nice creamy, melt in your mouth caramel bar or will it be a boring old scrap of paper in the shape of a raffle ticket?" He had a big cheeky grin on his face and so did I. I was so happy after being so disappointed. I felt like a kid in Willy Wonka's chocolate factory. I grabbed the raffle ticket out of the green bucket and immediately put it in the red bucket for the big draw. That was seven raffle tickets I'd collected; one for each week day plus two bonuses I'd scored along the way. As far as I could remember only one other person had got that many, so things were looking good.

We had about an hour to go before lunch but we had P.E. I love P.E. It's my second best subject. Computer Studies is my favorite because sometimes when we've finished our work we get to play games on the computer. There's nothing really exciting to play, only educational stuff but anything is better than work. Sometimes when Miss Egbutt is in a really good mood she lets us go on the internet and we can go on these really sick sites and play cool games. I wish we could go on Minecraft. That would be insane.

By the time we get back from P.E. Mr H has always counted all the raffle tickets and has the names of the eight kids with the most raffle tickets. Sometimes you can get a bonus for doing something really special. Sophie Delaney got an extra reward the other day because she went round with a bin at lunch time and picked up all the rubbish in the play area without being asked to by a teacher. Of course she didn't choose a raffle ticket; she chose a packet of M and M's. Not like she hadn't had enough chocolate for the week already. Whoops I'm being mean aren't I?

Some kids are such sucks though. They'll do anything to brown nose their way to be the teacher's pet. Or maybe it was the lure of the chocolate that made her grovel inside grubby rubbish bins. My Mom might reckon I'm obsessed with computer games but even I draw the line at picking up other people's rubbish just to get another chance at a raffle ticket. There is no way I would even think about picking up another kid's half eaten peanut butter and jelly sandwiches, snotty tissues or mouldy bits of orange peel that have been festering on the sides of the bin trying to escape.

James Hanson also got an extra reward when he represented our school at the Maths primary championships in the under 11's and came second. Mr H said that he deserved a really big reward for putting in such a good effort. I reckon there was probably only two in the competition. He chose a raffle ticket of course.

After we returned from P.E. Mr H gathered everyone on the mat again.
"Ok grade fivie wivies, let's have a gander at who our eight winners are this week. But before I do, I would like to make a very special announcement for those of you that are interested in the PlayStation club."

This sounded exciting. Anything to do with the PlayStation club was exciting but something in the tone of his voice made it sound as though this was going to be really awesome.

Chapter 8: The Big Game

"As some of you know my younger brother works at a game store; the job I always dreamed of doing but I never had the brains for, so I had to settle for becoming a teacher." He laughed heartily to himself but I had no idea why. "I have had the privilege of receiving a small donation from that store in the very shape of two PlayStation 3 games; the thrilling 'Need for Speed' and the notorious 'Superheros' which I am going to hold to ransom as the grand prize for a competition which shall otherwise be known as.... Drum roll please maestro." He patted a pencil tin beside him like he was in a rock band, and then in his deepest radio dj's voice said "The PlayStation Playoffs."

A few of the boys looked at each other with gleaming eyes. Matthew turned round and looked at me and tried to say something but I was too busy day-dreaming about the day I would walk in the front door with 'Need for Speed' and 'Superheroes' behind my back and surprise Mom. I had been asking for 'Need for Speed' ever since it came out. She just replies "Is it your birthday? Is it Christmas? Well what are you asking for? Money doesn't grow on trees you know."

One day I'm going to surprise her and plant a money seed and then I *will* grow some money and I can buy as many video games as I want to. But since I haven't found any money seeds yet, I've asked her if I can do jobs and save up for the game. She gives me 50 c every time I do a job. Whoopee do! So far I've only got eight dollars and fifty cents, which leaves only seventy two dollars and twenty cents to go. But if I could *win* the game, I could use my $8.50 on lollies instead.

“Rino, Rino pssst,” Matthew was trying to get my attention. “If you win it can I borrow it?”

“Matt Robinson!” Mr H boomed, “Do you have something you would like to share with the rest of the class or are you conducting a private consultation?” Matthew didn’t say anything. His cheeks just went a deep shade of beetroot as he turned back to the front. In trouble again. I hoped Mr H hadn’t realised whom he was talking to. I definitely didn’t want to be getting into trouble from now on. This was serious business. There was a PS game at stake now and it was going to be mine, all mine.

The lunch bell rang. “Ok, before you go I’d better let you know who the winning eight boys are this week. Whoops, I mean boys *or girls,* who can get their lunch and quickly come back to meet me in the computer room.” He rattled off the names and naturally I was right in there with exactly the same boys as the week before.

Of course there were no girls but he had to say it to be polite. “If you would like to hear the rules and conditions of the big competition please stay; if not, you may be dismissed for lunch.” All the girls got up. Some were mumbling how it wasn’t fair that they didn’t get any competitions. Others were saying they didn’t care about dumb old computer games anyway. They left and about ten or eleven boys remained behind. Only a few of them were a serious challenge to me. Most of the boys were pretty good players but Josh, Nigel, James and I were super good. Matty even posed a little bit of a threat sometimes.

“So,” he continued, “there will be four heats, starting at the end of next week with heat number one. So you all have a chance to get back in the draw by doing your work well and behaving perfectly next week. Do you hear that Matthew Robinson? If you win the first heat you must still make the criterion the following week and so on to play the other winners. If you win your heat but you fail to complete all criterion the following week you forfeit your place and someone else will take your place.”

Matthew put up his hand to ask what I thought might be an interesting question. “What does forfeit mean Mr H?” God he could be so dumb sometimes. Didn’t he remember when the Crazy cats used to forfeit us all the time in soccer? They said they couldn’t get enough players but we knew it was because they were scared of getting hammered by us. They weren’t the Crazy cats, they were the ‘scaredy cats’.

“It means you give it up, you give away the right to have that place in the final. Now in the third heat which is the last Friday of term two, the two top players will play off in the grand final and, as a special treat, anyone wishing to attend will be able to come and watch. We might even sell popcorn.”

There was a quiet buzz of excitement as all the boys dreamt about watching the grand final. I didn't want to think about going in to *watch.* I wanted to be the one in the hot seat playing.

"Ok boys, go and have your lunch and those of you that made it to the club this week need to be back here in ten minutes." We all rushed out. Everyone was trying to talk at the same time over the top of each other about the 'PlayStation Playoffs.' There'd never been anything so exciting at school as this.

I loved winning blue ribbons and red ribbons and even a green ribbon was something to be proud of in the swimming and athletics carnival. Once I even got a bronze medal for being third in the shotput, but I'd never had the chance to win a video game at school before. Gee Mr Higginbottom was a fantastic teacher even if he did have an embarrassing name.

"Matty," I called out as I raced out into the corridor. "You have to be really good next week so we can get in and verse each other."

"Yeah, but you'll beat me and then I'll be out." He pulled out his sandwich from the container. It was all squashed and something gooey was oozing out the sides. He looked disappointed. I looked at my own fresh meat sandwich and crunchy choc chip cookie next to the ice tray and immediately felt bad that I whinged to Mom that morning about having the same again. At least it was fresh.

And at least he was being kind to the ants and supplying them with their lunch for the day. I watched as a family of the little critters made their way to the sandwich fiesta.

“Yeah, but at least we can still play together first, and then you’ll be able to come and watch me in the final.” Mom always tells me to stop bragging; that I shouldn’t tell everybody how good I was all the time because it would appear as though I was full of myself. How can you be full of yourself? Does that mean you have to eat yourself up until you’re full? Sometimes my Mom says the weirdest things.

I hoped Mom was going to be excited for me when she heard about the competition. The thought crossed my mind that she might think it was a bad idea. She’d probably say something bizarre about it not being educational or something just as ridiculous and might not let me compete. What if she went to the principal and created a stir? The playoffs might get cancelled and maybe even the whole club could get abolished. I would so hate her if she did all that. My mind was racing a million miles an hour with crazy thoughts about my mother flinging her arms around like a hysterical butterfly in the principal's office and it didn't look pretty.

I made an executive decision as I munched on my cookie not to tell her. I was pretty sure she'd be thrilled about the whole thing but, I wasn't going to take any chances. Anyway, it would be more of a surprise to bring home the prize without anyone knowing what was going on. Although, my sister would probably hear all about it at school and tattle tale to Mom and Dad anyway.

But it didn't matter. All that mattered to me was that I made it into the playoffs and win. My Mom's dreary tones came back to me again, "It's not about winning Ryan, it's about playing fairly and having lots of fun. Blah blah blah blah." That might be all very well in sport but when 'Need for Speed' was up for grabs, winning was *everything*. This was war. **GAME ON BOYS!**

Chapter 9: And heat one is...

The following week dragged on as excitement built amongst the boys in the class. It was amazing how many boys stayed out of trouble and worked just that bit harder to get all their work completed and do well. Some even tried to do extra jobs and suck up to Mr H so they could get a bonus raffle ticket. I started to worry that there was too much competition, that I may not even make it into the first heat. What would happen if more than eight people had the same number of tickets in the barrel? Worse still, what happened if all the girls got the most? Some of them were even trying harder just to get up our noses. Sophie Delaney said she was going to win so she could sell it on eBay. She probably thought she would spend the eighty dollars she got on chocolate bars. As if she even stood a chance!

Mr Higginbottom said he would make sure that if more than eight kids got the same number of raffle tickets then he would make more heats on the first day. It's really hard to get any more than five though unless you get a bonus. He did give out a couple of extras. Cheryl Burbie (we call her 'furbie burbie' for short even though she doesn't like it) got any extra one for spelling the word 'rhinoceros'. Of course that didn't have anything to do with the fact that she looks a little bit like one. No-one else in the class got it right so the teacher thought she deserved a bonus. But Cheryl was no threat. Even if she got one hundred bonuses she wouldn't want to go in the club. She would just pick a hundred chocolate bars and stuff them all in her gob until a gigantic pimple full of caramel goo popped up on her nose.

Josh got an extra one for doing a violin recital at the Grandparent's day. He was the only one that volunteered. No-one else wanted to get up and play on their own. But then he can be such a goody goody. Unfortunately sometimes goody goodies can be excellent players too, so I could see he was going to be a bit of peril. Steve asked Mr H if he could polish his shoes one morning knowing he would get a bonus ticket for such a good deed.

Mr H keeps a tube of shoe polish in his draw in case someone's shoes look a bit scruffy. At the end of it his shoes were gleaming and Mr Higginbottom said, "Thankyou Steve. That was so nice of you to do that out of the kindness of your heart. Tell your Mom she's brought up a very kind and thoughtful young man," and he grabbed his coffee cup and left the room to go out and do his yard duty. I think the teachers aren't allowed to do their yard duty unless they have a coffee cup in their hands.

Steve was still kneeling on the ground and looking stunned. His chin had dropped and was almost touching the floor he was so flabbergasted. When I put that look on my face my Mom always says, "Close your mouth, are you trying to catch flies?" She's so weird at times. When I catch flies I use a piece of hair or fishing line. ***Not my mouth!! Yuk!***

By the time Friday had arrived we were all pretty nervous waiting to see who made the criteria for Friday and then who had the most raffle tickets to get through to the first heat. The teacher did his usual funny speech. “Ok grade fivie wivies, sitting up straight in your chairs, hands in front of you on the desk and all eyes at me. Ok you may now go to PE.”

There was hardly any movement, a few stunned heads turning but no-one moving from their chairs. Any other day there would have been a barrage of kids running towards the door like the running of the bulls in Spain. But because it was Friday *and* a very special Friday everyone was waiting to hear the news. Most kids had very confused looks on their faces, mine included.

“Only kidding, only kidding, now let’s get down to busy business. Ok the criteria for today is… and may I say I have made the conditions quite tough for this final day of this very exciting week, and may I also say what a great effort the whole grade has made in improving their behavior, and also the standard of work has been a credit to you all. You can all give yourselves a pat on the back." Of course everyone pretended to pat themselves on the shoulder while they giggled at each other. "And may I also say that…." He paused and looked around the classroom at the frustrated faces and heard the irate humming noise like angry bees coming in for an attack. "Ok, ok! I get the picture. Do you want me to tell you the criteria for today to see who will get something out of the green bucket?"

A few of the class answered yes impatiently.

"I didn't hear you!" he sung.

"YES!" we all screamed.

"Righteo then, you should have told me you wanted to know in the first place." He laughed again at his own bizarre humor. "The all important criteria is;

Number 1. As always you must not have got yourself into any trouble, big or small during the week. Well done Matthew Robinson," he chuckled.

"Number 2. All homework must have been handed in this morning.

Number 3. Your science experiment about worms should have been completed, written up and handed in this morning.

Number 4. The maths page on shapes all finished, and my final criteria for the day is…, you should have bought me a box of chocolates this morning because you know what they say 'a box of chocolates a day, gives you straight A's'. Ha ha ha ha," he bellowed to himself. "I'm so hilarious. And so, the winners are…." He paused as we all tried to make sense of what he had just said…… "Nobody. There are no winners because nobody bought me in a box of chocolates." He screwed up his face like a squashed snail and pretended he was going to cry, as the rest of us sat there bewildered. There were disappointed mutterings around the classroom as he came to our rescue.

"Alright we'll change the last one I suppose, but let it be a hint for you for next week. The final criteria is, yesterday's story on aliens must have been finished with a coloured drawing included *and* I hope none of the alien drawings look like me. And so……… the final green bucket winners are ...."

Chapter 10: And the Winners are.....

I held my breath really tight as he paused before he started rattling off the names. There were so many on the list and probably only two names to go when I finally heard, "and Ryan James and Jacob Anderson." I breathed out realising I was starting to go blue in the face because I was holding my breath for so long in anticipation. "Thank you ladies and germs. Those of you who have a raffle ticket please place it in the red bucket, those of you who took a chocolate bar, don't forget to share it with me, and those of you who missed out, SMARTEN UP! When you get back from PE, I will hopefully have counted the raffle tickets to see who has scored the most. Remember there has been a lot of extra competition this week, so if you normally get in the club, don't take it for granted that you will be in this time. Ok please form a line at the door then head off to your PE lesson."

No-one was really bothering to talk as we left which was pretty unusual as we were one of the most talkative classes apparently. Everyone was too distracted watching him start to count the tickets. Even the girls who really couldn't care less about the PS club were intrigued.

When we got back from PE I thought my guts were about to explode, not to mention my heart that was protruding through my ribcage beating unbelievably fast.

Mr H made a huge coughing sound and began to clear his throat as if he was making a speech to the president of the United States. "OK Dokey," he said, "this time took me quite a bit longer as there were lots of contenders lured to the competition because of the prize. The verdict is out and the winners of this week are....... and the winners are...........do you really want to know?" He said teasingly as the whole class screamed at him, "YES!" And Harry Burgess said, "Come on out with it mate."

"Ok first is ....Matthew Robinson, Josh Cameron, Jacob Anderson, Ryan James, Patrick Smithers and Tom Carter." I was in. I made it. After I heard my name, the rest was a blur. I didn't even hear him mention Nigel and James's name as well. I was in too much of an excited daze thinking about the first heat.

"Right," he said, "go and have ten minutes to eat your lunch and make sure you eat plenty of healthy stuff because you are going to need heaps of energy and loads of concentration. No junkie candy, ice-creams or bags of greasy fries for you guys. Ok!" As if our cafeteria would sell hot fries anyway.

"Yep," we all said as we ran out, grabbed our lunch bags and bolted down to the cafeteria. Competition or not, this was the one and only day of the whole week that my Mom allowed me to have an ice-cream at school and I *was not* going to miss out. I really didn't believe that one measly ice-cream would ruin my concentration anyway.

When we got into the computer room Mr Higginbottom and Miss Egbutt were in there chatting with their cups of coffee. Sometimes she comes in to watch us play. She says it's because she loves gaming but I think it's probably because she loves Mr H. When we see them outside in the playground doing yard duty together we always sing the song, "Egbutt and Higginbottom up a tree, k - i - s - s -i- n- g," but not when they can hear us of course. No-one really knows for sure, but the way they make googly eyes at each other is so insane, they must love each other.

It would be so weird if they got married because Miss Egbutt's name would change from being a butt to a bottom. My Mom got really mad at me when I told her that and she said I was being rude making fun of people's names. "People can't help what name they are given," she said, but I think I saw the corners of her eyes twinkling and wrinkling up into a little smile and her mouth was sort of twitching like she was trying not to laugh.

"Hey guys," Miss Egbutt greeted us. "That was really cool getting into the first heat. You must have worked pretty hard all week to deserve this."

"Yes they definitely have," interjected Mr H. "We don't want to waste any time though so let's make haste". I didn't really know what he meant by making haste. I didn't really want to make anything but he was moving towards his big, black case with the games inside so I just agreed. Mom told me later that it meant let's hurry.

"Now boys, there are eight of you here today so that means that four of you won't make it through to the heats next week. I need to know that if you are one of the ones that don't get through that you will act appropriately and maturely and take the loss like a true sportsman and not a baby in nappies." I think what he meant was that we couldn't crack it if we lost. So we all agreed. I didn't intend to lose anyway so it didn't matter.

"Ok. I have your names in a hat. Nigel, please draw a name out to see who you will battle today."

"What if I draw my own name out?" asked Nigel.

"Trust you to think of that. Well of course you draw again. It would be too easy to win if you had to play yourself now wouldn't it? Right! Go ahead, draw your combatant." Nigel slowly put his hand in like he was reaching in to a tank of piranhas in a feeding frenzy. When he pulled out the ticket without a piranha latching onto the end he quickly read it.

"Yeah easy peasy, I get to play Matthew."

"Oh," I mumbled disappointedly. I had wanted to play Matty but then on the other hand I didn't want to play him because when I beat him he would be out.

"Ok Jacob take a number." Jacob looked at Mr Higginbottom blankly.

"Where do I get a number from?" he said vaguely. For a smart kid he sure could be dumb sometimes.

"Pick a name stupid," said Nigel impatiently.

"Doh!" he said like Bart Simpson and laughed at his own stupidity. "Oh Ryan," he said after drawing my name out." I'm going to blitz you," he joked knowing full well he wouldn't.

"Now Josh dig in."

"How come he gets to go next?" Tom asked.

"Because he's prettier than you," and all the boys laughed at Mr. H as Josh drew out Tom's name.

"Ok now we'll see who the pretty one is," said Tom. "You're not gonna look so pretty when I've finished with you."

"Oooo I'm scared," teased Josh, egging Tom on.

"That means there are only two boys left. Patrick and James you will verse each other. Now boys here are the games you can choose from." He began to open his brief case.

"I don't suppose you got any Grand Theft Auto or Call of Duty in there?" asked Nigel hopefully.

"Don't be cheeky Nigel. You know M rated games are not allowed at school." He had a stern look on his face as he laid all the games out on the desk. I wanted to kick Nigel in the you-know-what for putting Mr H in a bad mood. He knows we're not allowed anything too violent, but he can't help himself opening up his big gob.

"If you can't agree on one then I'll have to choose for you. GAME ON BOYS! Choose your weapon."

It didn't take long for Jacob and me to agree on Star Wars Battlefront. I don't own that one at home but I've borrowed it from the DVD shop heaps of times and I've also discovered lots of unreal cheats on the internet when Mom thinks I'm looking up stuff for homework. Usually I'm allowed to have free 'screen time' as Mom calls it once a week on Wednesday after soccer training. But that means I use up all my time looking for cheats, and I never have any time left for Minecraft, so I like to make my own arrangements. Mom doesn't have to know everything.

We sat down in the bean bags in front of the TV. I was sitting on the one with a Homer Simpson cover on it. It had a little hole in it right where Homer's zip was in his jeans. It looked really funny because when I sat in it all the beans came flying out and it looked like he was peeing little white balls.

I loaded the game and we were off. I felt my neck start to thump like there was a little green gremlin inside with a hammer trying to escape out of my jugular vein. That's the main vein that goes from the brain to the heart. I learnt that in life education class by a giraffe called Harold driving a white van. I really wanted to win so bad it was making me nervous and we had to do it in the best of three games.

Our first game was ridiculously close. I chose the rebel troupers and Jacob chose the galactic empire. We chose cloud city during the galactic war era. After about fifteen minutes hard playing we had nearly the same point score and I thought I was going to lose until I got more life from the medical droid. It enabled me to take out the dark trouper, scout trooper and the imperial pilots making me the winner of the first game.

The second game came easily. I blitzed the troupers the whole way giving me a pretty cushy win for the first heat. Relief flooded every vein and artery in my body and gushed out into all my organs giving me a very happy feeling. We didn't even have to play the third match because I had already won two in a row.

I couldn't believe it. I had won the first heat. I knew I would, but here was still that little bit of worry lurking around. So did Josh, but Matty ost against Nigel who was looking pretty smug with himself. I felt like elling him that he had a piece of snot hanging on the end of his nose but I emembered my Mom's words telling me that just because some people are nean you shouldn't be mean back to them. Anyway I was too excited about winning to be mean.

Poor Patrick never stood a chance playing Dark Legends against James. James is king of Dark Legends and won both games easily. I couldn't wait until round two.

Chapter 11: The Pink Monster

The next week went really slow. Again everyone tried desperately to get into the club to watch the second round of heats. Even kids that weren't in the heats still wanted to get in the club to watch. It was the talk of the whole school. Any-one would have thought that the prize was a million dollars the way the excitement was buzzing. Our names even got into the school newsletter. "Typical," said my pain of a sister. "Trust you to get your name in the newsletter for computer games and not things that matter like athletics or school work."

"Well at least I got my name in. The only way you'd ever get your name in the newsletter is if they have a competition for the biggest loser."

"Mom!" she screamed. "Ryan's being mean!" My sister is such a dobber. She can never fight her own battles. She always has to bring Mom into it even though she's older and bigger than me, and fatter.

"So what's it all about this time?" Mom said with that impatient tone she gets when she's had enough of me and Lisa arguing. Mom knew about the PlayStation club but I hadn't told her about the competition and I wasn't about to give away too many details just in case.

"Just a competition, nothing much," I said casually as if I didn't care. As if!

"Nothing much? *Nothing much*? It must be pretty important if the principal is putting it in the school newsletter and saying that grade 5H is breaking all records in the good behavior department."

I didn't really agree with Mom though. It didn't take much to get in the newsletter. It was always full of boring bits of useless information like advertising a healthy fat free burger in the tuckshop, or announcing that the school had collected a thousand milk bottle tops or that there were ten thousand smelly jumpers in the lost property box.

"What's the prize?" she queried.

"Just a computer game."

"*Just* a computer game? I thought that would make you do a triple somersault in the air followed by a double back flip."

"Nah," I lied. "It's just another PlayStation game. Nothing to get excited about." Mom looked at me in shock and put her hand on my forehead. "Are you feeling alright? You're not coming down with anything are you?"

"Yeah", my sister piped up. "It's called weirdo disease."

"Mom!" I begged, pleading with my eyes to make her send the monster away.

"Lisa that's enough. She was only joking Ryan. Give her a break, it's her birthday soon."

"I know. She keeps reminding me like ten times a day."

"So what am I getting Mom?" Lisa butted in. "I've left a list on the fridge door just in case you need any help."

"Yes I know, you've told me one hundred and fifty–seven times and I saw it when you put it up three months ago. And I can tell you now you won't be getting a new mobile phone or an IPAD! But I will say that Daddy and I ..."

"Dad!" My sister angrily interrupted. "I do not call him Daddy. I'm not in kindy anymore."

"That's funny, 'cos you talk like you are, googa gagga," I teased.

"*Dad* and I have arranged a wonderful surprise that you both will really enjoy."

"Is it a dog?" Lisa's eyes lit up like a glow worm.

"No."

"A kitten?"

"No, sorry."

"A hamster?"

"Lisa…"

"A goldfish? Frog? Turtle? A lady bug? Anything alive?" Lisa sounded like she was playing a game of charades and starting to look desperate.

"Go on, tell her Mom. It's an ant." I couldn't help stirring Lisa up.

"Mom it's not an ant is it?" she said in her most whiney voice.

"Yeah," I said, "and it's not only one ant it's a whole nest of them and they're big juicy green ants and they're going to bite you all over."

"Don't be silly Ryan! Why do you do this to your sister? Of course it's not a green ant Lisa. It's a pink ant with purple spots." Mom laughed at her own joke as Volcano Lisa nearly erupted into a mass of slimy larva.

"Oh Lisa, I'm only joking. It's *nothing* alive. It's not a pet and that's all I'm going to say. Except you will both get a lot of enjoyment out of it."

"It's ok Mom, you don't have to do anything for me on Lisa's birthday. I'll be ok." I knew that the day of her birthday was going to be the biggest day in my life, better than any old birthday present. It was the day of the PlayStation playoffs grand final, but I didn't tell them that. While Lisa was pampering herself in new sparkly pink lip gloss and tizzying her hair with pink butterflies and wearing new pink skirts and pink shirts to match her new pink undies, I'd be happy playing my brand new game oblivious to the attention seeking pink alien inhabiting our house.

It wasn't just the fact that I could win the game; it was more than that. Whoever won the playoffs would be the hero of our grade. Possibly even the hero of the school even if just for a little while. I would become so popular if I was the winner.

Chapter 12: Stalking Gremlins

I could already sense my popularity increasing when it came to the day of the second heats. Lots of people were coming up to me wishing me good luck.

"You're going to blitz 'em," said Craig Jenkins. He was one of the coolest boys in our class. Everyone liked him, even the girls. Craig liked the girls too which is pretty gruesome. He tried to get into the playoffs but he always gets into trouble for talking too much. He can't help it though. He's so popular everyone wants to talk to him all the time. I think he's even got a girlfriend in sixth grade. Yuk! It's bad enough having a girlfriend, but a sixth grader! Some of them even have those pointy bits and they have to wear bras. ***DoubleYuk!***

"Thanks," I whispered as Mr Higginbottom was just about to announce who got the final raffle tickets for Friday and I didn't want to blow my chances by getting into trouble for talking at the last minute.

"Let's have a lookie at the criteria for today and we'll see if those boys desperate to play in their second heat make the cut," he announced.

"Ok number one is as always, you must not have been in any trouble this week in any shape or form, be it big or little, wide or fat, stumpy or grumpy.
Number 2. All sums in your Maths book completed from pages 38 to 44.
Number 3. Ah let's see, Ten out of ten for the spelling test today,
Number 4. Homework must have been handed in this morning and two chapters of Delta Quest read last night. Oh yes and one tricky one, you must

be up to at least page 5 in your Ocean Life work book. I don't think that is an unreasonable request considering you've had three afternoons to work on it."

There was a lot of disgruntled moans and screwed-up faces coming from the class suggesting that a lot of people weren't up to page 5.

"Now, now, if you'd worked as hard as you were supposed to, you would easily be up to page seven so no mumbling and grumbling from the peanut gallery please. So …. Is that enough or would you like one more criteria?"

Everyone shouted "no more" at the same time.

"Ok, so if I look at my little black book here, the people that *did* meet all the criteria and will get a raffle ticket or chocolate bar today are….." He paused. It was like watching 'Who wants to be a millionaire' on T.V. when it goes to an ad break just before you find out if the contestant got it right or not. He was always pausing and keeping us waiting.

That little gremlin started thumping inside my jugular vein again. What if I didn't make it into the second heats because of some silly little thing? I thought I had completed everything but I couldn't remember if I was up to page four or five of the Oceans work book. The gremlin starting charging through my body like it was on a rampage, ripping at my veins and causing blood to pulsate in rapid torrents throughout my body. I wished Mr H would hurry up and say the names so I could stop the gory images infiltrating my head.

"They are, they are …H'mm should I tell you now or should I keep you in suspense until after lunch?" He was teasing us, but he quickly called out the names before anyone had a chance to explode.

"Sophie, Kristy, Josh, Ryan, Sarah, Nigel, Jacob, Ella, James, Joel, Melanie and Tom. Come up and take your pick out of the green bucket. If you wish to select a chocolate bar as your grand prize please come up and do so now." Of course the girls went up and grabbed chocolates.
"What about you Ryan? Wouldn't you like to select one of these yummy, mouth-watering Kit Kats for your prize? Nigel? What about you Josh, you don't want to go to the computer room do you?" Mr Higginbottom teased. He knew that there would be no tempting the four winners of heat one away from heat two. The other boys also wanted raffle tickets so they could try and get in to have a bit of a sticky beak at the finals.
"You know the drill kids. Chocolate - eat, ticket - red bin. Peter you can come up here and tell the rest of the class a joke while these kids are organising their prizes. You always seem to have a lot to say for yourself, now's your chance."

Peter bounded up to the front of the class. He definitely wasn't a shy kid. He stood up the front with a big cheesy grin on his face. "Ummm umm ah," he began, not knowing what to say.
"Well that's a very funny joke Peter," Mr Higginbotton said, "but have you got a joke with some words that we might recognise?"
"Oh yeah I remember one now. Why did the poo…"
Mr H interrupted. "One that doesn't have any words that sound like poo, look like poo or smell like poo please Peter. Try again."
"Ok. Ahhhh……" He was again lost for words again. "Oh I know. Why did the toilet paper roll down the hill?"

No-one in the class knew the answer, but someone yelled out, "that joke smells like poo, Mr Higginbottom."
The whole class roared with laughter. "Ok enough! What's the answer Peter?"
"Because it wanted to get to the bottom." The class erupted into peals of laughter again.
"Alrighty then, settle down. Thankyou Peter for your agh.....intelligent and witty sharing of information. Off to PE everyone and when you return I will have this week's raffle tickets counted."

Mr Higginbottom's words became a blur as he rambled on again about having a big lunch and going to the toilet. Who could even think about doing a pee at a time like this? I was too excited about winning the next heat and worried about who I would have to battle against. If only, if only I could just get through the next heat, I knew the glory would be all mine and I would be one game away from claiming the championships. But somewhere deep inside me a terrible feeling was looming. The mighty gremlin was starting to stalk me again.

Chapter 13: Heat 2

I needn't have been so worried. If I thought heat one had been pretty easy, heat two was even easier. Of course I had enough raffle tickets to get into the playoffs and so did Nigel, Josh and James. There was no way we weren't getting in.

I had to verse Josh and I totally flogged him. He didn't stand a chance from the moment I took out ten of his soldiers and four of his tanks in the first five minutes. He never came anywhere near my score for both the matches. Again I won two in a row so the third game was only for fun though Josh was being a bit of a sook through it, so it wasn't much fun. Mr H had to remind him about good sportsmanship.

The match between James and Nigel was insanely close. They had only just started their second match when Josh and I had finished, so we got to watch the rest. It was so exciting. Nigel refused to play Dark Legends because he knew James was so good at it and in the end Nigel beat him in the third game of Dragon Ball Z. In the last match James couldn't even land a hit on Nigel because he was using his best character. After dodging a lot of attacks from James, Nige ducked under a punch and knocked him to the floor. I didn't know whether to be happy or sad. I was sad because James lost but happy that we didn't have to verse each other. But I was really, really sad because it meant that I had to verse 'nasty Nige' in the final. If there was one person who could probably beat me, it was him. What a week it was going to be.

Chapter 14: The Big Day Looms

The night before the big day, Mom and I had to go to the shops to buy Lisa's birthday present. She was at her stinky girlfriend's house supposedly doing homework but probably putting lipstick on their fingernails and nail polish on their eyelids or something dumb like that. They'd be making their hair look stupid with fluffy bits of junk hanging out all over the place while they talked about their boyfriends. How any boy in sixth grade would ever like them beats me. Girls are so weird sometimes.

Mom asked me if there was anything special I wanted to get Lisa. I felt like saying a tin of smelly dog food mixed with a spoon of bat poo sprinkled over cats vomit. Yuk! But instead I just said, "maybe a doll?"

"Don't you think she's got enough dolls?" Mom said. "And anyway, I think she's getting a bit too old for dolls don't you?"

I didn't answer because we'd just entered the store and my attention was snatched by something out of the corner of my hungry eyes. It was like some royal king sitting on his throne reigning supremely over the kingdom. It was the most fantastic thing I'd ever seen in my whole ten years of life; the PlayStation 4 console.

"Mom!" I said excitedly, losing control of myself. "It's only $55. Can we get it? Pleeeease. I promise I'll be really good. I'll do some jobs and promise not to be mean to Lisa any more. I'll do anything you want; I'll even pick up dog poo for the neighbors."

“Ryan, have a closer look at the price. It’s not $55. It’s $555, and I don’t care whether you’re the most perfect boy in the whole country, the whole world or the whole solar system for that matter, you will not be getting a PS 4 while it has a price tag like that on it. In fact, even if it was half price you still wouldn’t be getting it.”

“Why not?”

“Because we can’t afford it." I knew what was coming next. “Money doesn’t grow on trees you know.”

“I know, I know. You’ve told me like a million times.” But I wasn’t too disappointed. I had the ‘playoffs’ grand final to think about. While Mom went and found some boring pink things for Lisa, I went and looked at the computer games, had a turn at a few display consoles, and thought about my strategies for the next day.

That night it took forever to get to sleep. I lay in my bed under my Star Wars doona and pretended I was asleep when I heard Mom coming to check on me. I couldn’t stop thinking about the next day. I had my cheats that I got from the internet tucked nicely underneath the covers looking at them with the torch. I quickly snuck in five minutes of zombie blasting, pig taming and built a big shopping centre on Minecraft, and then went back to revising my cheats.

Lisa kept calling out to Mom for things, pretending she was thirsty, saying she was cold or needing to tell Mom something important. She obviously couldn't sleep either. Just because it was her birthday the next day, she was playing on it. Every time Mom came past to see what she wanted, I quickly snapped my torch off or she would have taken it away from me.

Finally at long last I drifted off into a restless sleep full of dreams of PlayStations, Minecraft, light sabres and army men.

Chapter 15: Big, Bad Dreams

It felt like I'd been sleeping all night when I started to have the weirdest dream. It felt so real as though I was right there actually experiencing it. I suppose that's what dreams are like though.

I could feel myself sitting on a warm sandy beach with the sun shining on me making me feel as snugly as a piece of toast, when all of a sudden two monstrous furry hands that looked like they belonged to a gigantic troll reached down and scooped me off the sand and threw me onto its hairy shoulders. The sun was immediately eclipsed by a blanket of darkness and I felt my dwarfed body tingle with the cold as the creature absconded with me into the night air. I could hear a strange wailing noise coming from somewhere. It was an eerie, gurgling sound trying to utter some unintelligible words.

As I started to waken, the words became clearer and I could hear myself shouting, "No, no, no!" The sound was coming from me! I was screaming out in my sleep objecting to the monster-like creature taking me away from the warmth of the beach, but it refused to stop. Instead it dropped me into some transportation enclosure, tied me up with a strap and offered me some morsels of food in consolation.

The next thing I knew, everything was moving fast, rushing past me like a space craft zooming into outer space, faster and faster. For awhile I felt myself drift off into a coma like state again but was woken by the presence of a strange alien next to me, bumping into me, taunting me and calling my ame in a high pitched whine. "Ryan, Ryan." It kept bumping and tapping ny face and touching my ears. My arms started to flap as I tried to fight it ff and my eyes squinted as a bright pink light started to infiltrate the larkness. I looked up and saw the alien looking down at me. It was big and cary, it was weird and it was the ugliest vision I had ever seen. It looked xactly like my sister.

"Aghhhhhhhhhh!" I screamed as I saw its big tentacles reach out to try and suffocate me. I was just about to reach for my laser gun and my triple whammy light saber to pelt the thing with a hail of gunfire when it spoke to me and wrapped its slimy limbs around my petrified neck.

"Give me a hug for my birthday," it said in a squeaky voice. I stared at the creature that looked scarily like my sister. I focused my eyes on its big ugly face and searched for clues. I looked harder and harder as my eyes began to open wide.

"Aghhhhhhhh," I screamed again when I realised that the alien was in actual fact *not* an alien who looked like my sister, but in fact *was* my sister who looked like an alien. I fearfully looked around my surrounds, and to my horror realised we were both sitting squashed in the back seat of my parent's car with a smelly picnic basket squeezed between the two of us travelling along some highway.

Aaaaaaaghhhhhhh !

“Good morning darling,” I heard my Mothers chirpy voice come from the front seat. “Wish your sister a happy birthday.”

I looked at her. I looked at my sister and I looked at my Dad who was happily driving the car and whistling cheerily. I wondered if we were already on the way to school and whether I had slept through the getting ready bit. I looked down and saw I was still in my pj’s.

“No, no, no!” I started to panic uncontrollably. “What’s going on? Where are we going? Why aren’t we at home getting ready for school? I can’t go to school in my pj’s. MOM?”

Ryan settle down. It's all ok. Lisa, why don't you tell him about the birthday surprise?"

"We're going to Movie World for *my* birthday and even though it's not your birthday, you still get to come *and* you get to miss out on school because it's *my* birthday. So you can thank me later with some candy. Mom, why *do* we have to bring Ryan? Why should he miss out on school when it's *my* birthday? It's not his. I never got to miss out on school when it was his birthday."

"Because he's your brother Lisa and you love him and want him to be part of your birthday celebrations and we're going to have lots of fun as a whole family this weekend. Isn't that right Ryan?"

I WAS DUMFOUNDED! I was as flabbergasted and as panic-stricken as a guppy fish coming face-to-face with a great white shark. I couldn't believe my disastrous luck and I couldn't open my mouth. It was glued to my gums. I felt like my brain was moving in slow motion getting ready to erupt like a volcanic explosion spewing molten lava into the atmosphere.

"Ryan, Ryan, aren't you excited? Did you hear what I said? We're going to MOVIE WORLD," she shouted, "and you get to miss a whole day of school all because of me."

"NOOOOO!" I screamed. "I am *not* excited. Take me back. I want to go to school. It's a school day, take me back. I can't miss school today!" I was beginning to realise the whole truth of what was happening. It was the day of the playoffs grand final, and I was hurtling down the highway at 100 kilometres per hour in the opposite direction when I should have been standing in front of the TV, brushing my teeth and watching Prank Patrol on TV on ***the*** most important day of the whole year, if not the most important day of my whole life.

Instead, these unimaginable creatures who called themselves my loving family had ripped me from my cosy bed, kidnapped me while the cold night air still lingered before day break and whisked me off unknowingly while I slept. To make matters worse they left me exposed to the world with my Thomas the Tank engine pyjamas still on. If anyone saw me in those, I'd be history. I would be so embarrassed.

"Now I *know* he's really, *really* gone all weirdo on us. How can he want to go to school when we're going to Movie World?" My sister just had to throw her bit in. Right about then, I wished there was a massive earthquake and the road cracked in a lightning shaped form and swallowed her up whole like a dinosaur slurping down his breakfast. It was all her fault we were heading in the opposite direction to school.

"Mom I want to go back," I pleaded in my sweetest voice. "Please I want to go to school today. I CAN'T MISS SCHOOL!"

"What on earth's got into you today? I know you love school but it's only one day. You're in fifth grade Ryan. It's not like you're missing out on your twelfth grade finals. *And* we're going to Movie World for goodness sake. Anyone would think we're forcing you to take the day off to go to the dump to search for dinosaur bones." Actually that would probably be good fun, but not on this day, *not* grand final day.

"Now say happy birthday to your sister and stop being bad-mannered and inappreciative." Sometimes Mom sounded like a cd stuck on a scratch saying the same thing over and over. She was always going on about being more appreciative.

"Happy birthday," I begrudgingly mumbled into my chest.

"I can't hear you," my smarty pants sister snarled.

"HAPPY BIRTHDAY!" I yelled into her ears. "Mom I need to go back now. Please, I have to go to school today."

"Ryan just settle down and stop this ridiculous behavior. We're half an hour from the Gold Coast. We're going to stop at Maccas and have breakfast and you and Lisa can get dressed. We should be at Movie World by 9.30 and you'll forget all your woes and troubles. So pull yourself together and get a grip. That's just the way things are and I don't want to hear another word unless it's a happy one."

She started talking in that low voice to Dad, the one she uses when she's trying to make out it's only for Dad's ears but she really wants us to hear. "I don't know what's got into that boy. Most kids would think it's Christmas getting to go to Movie World on a school day. I don't know what's so exciting at school today but I'm sure it can wait."

"That's just it. It won't wait. It's today Mom. It's the grand final of the PlayStation playoffs, remember in the news letter. I'm in the final today. I could win two games." I said as I started to break down into a blubbering mess.

"Oh Ryan, why didn't you tell us?"

"I did."

"When?"

"Just then. Oh Mom I wanted it to be a surprise so I could just come home with the game and show you. Now do you understand?"

"Yes I do understand why you feel that way. I guess that would have been a little bit exciting." OMG! My Mother, did she live under a rock? A *little* bit exciting. *A little bit exciting*? Was she for real?

"So can you please turn the car around and go back now? " I asked with relief filtering through my veins.

"It's a great shame Ryan darling, but no dear of course we can't turn the car around and go back." She chuckled to herself and looked at Dad.

"It's not that you can't, you won't, because you like her more than me!" I was starting to get mad and beginning to blubber again. Nothing, *nothing* in the whole world could have felt worse than that moment.

Right about that time everyone would be going eagerly into class. Matthew and Josh would be looking for me and wondering where I was. Nigel the mean kid would be looking smugly at everyone with that cheesy smile knowing he was about to win the most prestigious competition to ever exist without even trying.

Then an even worse thought hit me. What if Mr Higginbottom replaced me with Josh and he got a chance to win? That would be worse. Then again, if I couldn't win, I would rather Josh beat Nigel. I started to sob quietly with my head buried in the car door, and then I was full on bawling like a big dumb girl. I couldn't help it and my sister had to add to my misery.

You sure are such a big baby. Baby, baby," she chanted, taunting me when was at my lowest.

'Lisa just leave him. Ryan things aren't really that bad. Sometimes they eem worse than what they really are. In fact sometimes when things seem eally bad, something really good happens out of the blue to make you forget he bad things, like the fact that we're going to Movie World."

What would my Mom know? How could anything good come out of missing he grand final? The only thing that was likely to happen is that I would become known as a loser, a big wimp who was too scared to turn up to beat the snotty nosed, nasty Nige.

I cried so hard, I drifted back into a world of grief-stricken slumber. It only seemed about five minutes had passed when I woke to find the car pulling into the McDonald's car park. All I could think about was that I had a very big desire to pee.

During my sleep I'd somehow stopped crying but my tears had dried into what felt like cracked snot all over my face. With my warm pyjamas on, I felt like a ridiculous swamp monster emerging from the deep, covered in slime, wearing baggie Thomas the tank flannelettes. Mom helped me get dressed. The autumn sun was starting to warm the morning, and sitting in the sun drenched car felt like a sauna. I was sizzling like a sausage on a bbq so I was glad when Mom helped me into my boardies and Bart Simpson singlet.

I looked up and saw the big golden M's looming down, beckoning me to come in. I hadn't felt hungry when I was first rudely awoken but after the trauma I had endured I supposed I could force down a bacon and egg muffin with some pancakes. It wouldn't make me any happier though but at least it would get rid of the squirmy, gnawing feeling in my tummy.

Mom and Dad are usually pretty stingy when it comes to buying fast food so I thought I may as well take up the opportunity while it was there. Mom says we don't buy it much because she's looking after our health and our bodies by not putting in too much junk. What would she know?

I reckon Macca's is pretty healthy anyway. Even the Big Macs contain food from most of the five healthy food groups. The roll is from the bread group and the meat patty is meat. Cheese is from the dairy group and the veggie group is represented by lettuce and the green pickle that no-one ever eats. Even the fries are made from potatoes. So how much healthier does she want it to be?

So I thought while we were there, I may as well force myself in and enjoy some of the five food groups. I couldn't think which group the pancakes came under though.

Chapter 16: Movie World vs the Playoffs

By the time we got to the grand entrance of Movie World, the playoff's grand final had faded into the background of my brain and I was starting to get excited about going on the roller coaster and the Batman ride. The last time we had gone to Movie World I was only a toddler and had been too little to go on anything scary. They had little statues of movie characters next to each ride and if you weren't as tall as they were you couldn't go on the ride. To be honest, back then I was too scared to go on anything anyway. Mom said when they tried to get me on the Scooby Doo ride, little China men would have heard me screaming in China. I think the only ride I went on all day was the merry go round. Even then I didn't dare go on top of a horse that bobbed up and down. I sat in the safety of a stationary boat.

But this time I was going to go on everything. Mom said because it was a school day there might not be many queues so we could have as many turns as we wanted on everything.

When we were finally at the ticket box I felt a stray smile sneaking up all over my face and taking over my grumpy frown. I tried to keep feeling sad about the playoffs, but the lure of Movie World was starting to take over me like a parasitic alien inhabiting his victim. No matter how I tried to fight the betrayal, the feelings of thrilling anticipation won over until in the end I let it possess me and I began to feel really excited. I couldn't wait to get to the new Superman ride first.

As I walked through the number three gate and paid the admission, Dad made a joke to the lady about having to rob a bank just to afford to come to Movie World. Dad's always cracking sick jokes to people he doesn't know. Just as Mom started to roll her eyes at Dad, a huge siren started sounding and flashing lights began illuminating over the gate we were entering.

At first I thought it was a fire alarm or something even more threatening like a bomb scare. Mom also looked worried so that made me even more scared until the lady at the ticket booth said with a big toothy grin, "Congratulations young man you've won. As part of our twenty year celebrations this week we are giving away a major prize each day to the 20th visitor through the gates and you, young man, are our lucky winner for today." It looked as though she was looking straight at me. I turned around to see if there was some other boy that she was talking to standing behind me, but apart from the other trillion people queuing up, there wasn't anyone right behind.

I'd won. I'd won a prize for the first time in my life. I immediately hoped it was going to be something cool like a batman toy or a batman show bag and not just a hotdog or some other junk food voucher that Mom wouldn't approve of. I'd have to share it with Lisa and I was still full from Macca's breakfast anyway.

"Hello you lucky thing, what's your name?" She was still looking at me all sparkly eyed, so I answered.

"Ryan James." She answered me so it must have been for real.

Well Ryan I am pleased to tell you that today's prize is a pretty special ne." She looked at my Mom and Dad who were beaming excitedly at me. 'hey definitely thought it was going to be more than hotdog and fries. 'Mr and Mrs James?" she queried. "You're Ryan's parents? I just need to get some details from you, and your super prize will be here for collection when you're ready to leave. Come with me this way." She put up a sign saying back in one minute. The man behind me got a bit grumpy and I heard his wife say, "Don't get your knickers in a knot," which is a really peculiar thing to say. As if you could get your knickers in a knot when you're wearing them, grumpy or not!

The very nice lady (well I thought she was very nice because she was going to give us something for free) ushered us into an office. Lisa didn't want to come in. She was starting to get all sulky because she was customer number nineteen and didn't win the prize. If you ask me it serves her right for pushing me out of the way just so she could hold Dad's hand in the line. Most of the stuff at Movie World is boy stuff anyway like Batman, Superman and Lethal weapon things so I don't know why she was so jealous. Even most of the Harry Potter stuff is for boys. I hoped the prize wasn't going to be some big, fluffy tweety bird because then I really would want to give it to Lisa.

Anyway Mrs Very Nice Lady gave Mom and Dad some forms to fill out. They chatted for a moment. I think Dad made a few crazy jokes but I wasn't really listening. I was too busy trying to guess what the prize might be. I was really hoping for the Batman show bag because then you get lots of different things to play with, including a mini bat mobile. I remember Matty bringing one for show and tell last year after his holiday. It was really awesome.

“Would you like to know what your prize is before you enjoy the day or keep it a surprise for the end of the day?”

“YES! I would love to know.” I didn’t hesitate in answering as my mom and Dad both simultaneously said, “NO!” I wanted to know straight away. I couldn’t bear the suspense all day but Dad was very insistent we would wait the whoooooooole day.

“We’ll definitely wait until the end of the day. It will give you something to look forward to,” he said giving me one of those looks, “and it will help us to drag him away from the lethal weapon,” he said with a wink to Mrs Very Nice Lady. “Come on let’s go. Thankyou very much Amy. It’s been a pleasure doing business with you.”

“Have a great day,” she replied, “and you will absolutely be mad about your prize,” she said, looking at me.

“Why does he have to get the prize? It’s my birthday!” Lisa whinged as we left the office.

“Lisa I’m sure Ryan will share it with you, won’t you Ryan?”

“Depends if she’s nice to me or not. And it depends what it is. If it’s some big fluffy toy from Looney Toons then she can have it all to herself.”

Dad gave Mom a wink when he thought I wasn’t looking. I had no idea what that meant but usually when Dad winks at Mom it’s because they’ve got some secret going.

WELCOME TO
MOVIE WORLD

Chapter 17: Cool Riders

The rest of the day at Movie World was sick as. Lisa and I both forgot that we started our days in the poo. I had pretty much forgotten all about the play offs by the time I had my first ride on the Justice League ride. It was ancient history. During the day whenever the thought entered my brain space fleetingly, it was quickly pushed out through my earhole and out into the thin air by the temptation of another thrill seeking ride.

There were heaps of other cool rides and lots of free stuff because of their birthday celebrations. I got to go on the Batman ride three times and I didn't have to queue up once. Mom was right about the queues. The first time I was a bit scared and I nearly didn't go on it but Lisa talked me into it. She was awesome. She went on absolutely everything with me. Lisa proved to be a real thrill seeker when it came to going on the rides. I thought being a girl she would chicken out of everything except the Looney tunes corner but she was braver than me sometimes, but I didn't tell her that. Her head already resembles a bratz doll it's so big.

She kept making me go on everything again and again and again.

In the end my tummy felt like it had been taken over by a frenzy of wriggling worms doing cartwheels at a gymnastics carnival. Imagine a gymnastics carnival for worms. Don't know how they'd do a handstand though.

Lisa's pretty cool sometimes I guess. Dad went on some rides too but Mom didn't. She said someone had to do the hard job of staying with the bags. At lunch time I thought she might have pulled out the winning prize - free hotdog vouchers, but instead she pulled out smelly egg sandwiches made from bread that resembled soggy toast. Normally I love egg sandwiches but not when they've been squished at the bottom of a hot back pack for three hours getting all mushy as they rub up and down Dad's back.

At that point I would have been quite happy to accept hotdog vouchers as my winning prize but Mom assured me that the real prize was waiting back at the front office and would probably be a lot more exciting than hot dogs.

"No birthday cake Mom?" asked Lisa, returning to her whinging ways for a fleeting moment.

"Well it was a bit difficult to pack one in the back pack Lisa, but I'm sure we can come up with something at the apartment."

Judging by the condition of the sandwiches I was pretty glad Mom didn't pack a birthday cake. It would have been like one big fat pancake with pink icing.

By the end of the day we were all pretty stuffed, but Mom said we had to find some more energy to go out for supper for Lisa's birthday so we had to go home at 4 o'clock to rest even though the gates didn't close until five. Lisa and I started to complain that we hadn't had enough rides but then I remembered the prize waiting for me at the front gate, so I was happy to leave. Lisa had to be bribed with an ice-cream before we could finally find out what the mysterious prize was waiting for me.

Back at the entrance, the nice lady Amy had gone home for the day so I started to panic that the new lady might not know anything about the prize or where it was. When Dad told her who we were, her face lit up immediately as though we were really important people. "Oh so you're oday's lucky winner. Well you're going to have heaps of fun with this I can ust see." She was looking straight at me as if she already knew I was the vinner. She asked Dad to sign some papers and asked him for some dentification. Then she handed over the hugest box with a big ribbon tied around it. There weren't any words written on it to give away any clues.

I was just about to leave the office when Mom pulled one of her angry faces. Dad says she carries around a suitcase full of different faces depending on what's happening. "Ryan, aren't you forgetting something?" I looked around for something I'd forgotten.

"No, Dad's got the box," I replied.

"Aren't you forgetting to say something?"

"Oh yeah thanks heaps Mom."

"Not to me silly."

"Oh yeah, sorry." I was so used to saying thanks to Mom all the time. I turned to the lady who was beaming brightly at me. "Thank you very much, god blesses you."

Mom whispered in my ear," Ryan it's lovely to say that but you don't have to say god bless you every time you thank someone. Now let's go and have a look at this present."

"Let's wait until we get back to the hotel to open the prize," Dad butted in as he began loading it into the boot.

"No! No Dad please can I open it here. I've been waiting all day patiently." I began jumping up and down tugging on Dad's shirt. I knew that would make him give in because he hates it when I do that.

"Oh alright, I suppose you've waited long enough. Come on let's get in the back seat and have a look." He put the box in the back and I jumped in beside it.

"Watch it!" shouted Lisa as I accidentally brushed past her to get in. "Don't push. Mom, he's pushing me."

I tried to rip the box open but it wouldn't budge. Dad got his pen knife and slit the taping down the side.

"Oh My God!" were the only words that came out of my mouth.

Chapter 18: Heaven in a Box

"OH MY GOD! OH MY GOD!" I couldn't think of anything else to say.
"I thought you said not to use the lord's name in vain," said the whining blob of a sister, but her futile words were just like smelly gas vaporising into the atmosphere to me. My heart froze and my legs went all wobbly. I felt like a jelly fish doing the Macarena, which is sort of a dance. Dad calls it the macaroni and my legs definitely resembled soggy macaroni right then.

Inside the plain brown box was a white box with a very familiar brand name on the side. It could only mean one thing. I grabbed at it like a seagull in a frenzied attack on sandy bread crusts at the beach, and pulled it out.

"OMG! OMG!" I kept saying when I saw the sacred words and graphics on the side of the box. "Thankyou God. Thankyou sooooooo much." I raced back to the office where the lady had given me this wonderful miracle wrapped up in a box. I could hear Mom screaming out in her normal shrill tone, "Careful, watch the road!" She didn't have to worry. I wasn't about to go head to head with a bus and leave my body imprint on it now that I had won that prize.

"Ryan, where are you going?" Dad called out.

I burst into the office. "Thankyou so much," I said to the bewildered lady. I felt like hugging her which was pretty scary as I hate hugging girls, but I did anyway. I think she was a little bit dumbfounded.

Then I raced back out to my heavenly treasure waiting for me. Mom and Dad were standing up leaning against the car with really cheesy grins on their faces. Dad's smile went from one ear all the way round to his other ear. I think he was just as excited as I was. Lisa of course was slumped over the back seat with a huge grumpy look on her face pretending to be asleep. Girls are so weird. They just can't stand not being the centre of attention all the time, especially when it's their birthday.

Again I pulled the white box out and hugged it tightly like a precious, new born baby. I couldn't believe it. I was going to be the first boy in Fifth grade, maybe even in the whole school to own this.

Chapter 19: The luckiest Boy in the World

It was all mine. Nearly six hundred dollars worth. It was the best day of my whole life. I was now the proud owner of a PlayStation 4. "I own a PlayStation 4," I kept saying it to myself, because I couldn't believe it was true. I was the luckiest person that ever roamed the earth.

"Have you looked in the bottom of the box?" Dad said as he motioned towards the brown box? Puzzled I looked inside and on the bottom was not one, not two, but five games and one girlie one. Maybe if Lisa was nice to me I'd let her have that one. I started hyperventilating I was so excited.

"Mom can we forget about staying the weekend and just go home now?" I knew what her answer would be but all I wanted to do was go home and set the console up on our big 72 inch TV.

"Absolutely not young man! We've paid for the hotel and we are here to celebrate Lisa's birthday and that's what we're doing."

"Ok! Ok, ok," I said. It was worth a try, but I knew I'd been very lucky so I wasn't going to push my luck further.

"Well Dad can you set it up in the hotel room?"

"Noooo!" Dad said. "Of course not. We'd end up wrecking all the settings in a TV that doesn't belong to us."

"Pleeeeeeease," I said starting to get desperate. I reminded myself of how Lisa sounded when she put on one of her whiney voices begging for a second cupcake. It's no wonder she's starting to get pimples, they always give into her.

“Ryan we’ve given you the answer.” Dad put on one of his stern looks that meant *‘don’t say another word or you might not live to tell the tale.’*

“Now don’t ruin a wonderful thing by wanting more. Be happy and content with what you’ve been given. When we get it home tomorrow as soon as we’ve unpacked I’ll set it up for you. Unless Mom wants to do all the unpacking by herself, then we can get started straight away, hey love?”

He looked at Mom. And Mom shot him one of *her* looks that said *‘don’t you even dare think about it.’* And he kissed her on the head. Yuk!

“So do we have a deal?” Dad said to me.

I didn’t answer.

“DEAL?” he raised his voice.

“Ok deal,” I said, but I didn’t know how I was going to get through the next twenty-four hours without being able to set up my precious console.

Mom and Dad have this habit of bringing me down when things are looking really great. But I suppose they had a point. It *was* Lisa’s birthday and this weekend *was* for her. It was the most exciting day in my whole ten years and I wasn’t going to let anything ruin it for me. Even when Santa Claus brought my PlayStation 2 to the house and got it stuck in the chimney didn’t come close to this.

Chapter 20: Unbelievable

couldn't wait to get to school on Monday to tell everyone about my prize. I didn't even remember to ask about the play offs until Matthew greeted me at the gate. “What happened to you on Friday? Are you better now?”

“What?”

“You missed the grand final ‘cos you were sick didn't you? You must have been so sick you had to go to your own funeral to have missed that.”

“Oh yeah, Doh! I nearly forgot. No I wasn't sick. I was at Movie World.”

“Oh sick man, that's cool. Still, I can't believe you went on the day of the grand final.”

“Yeah I know. Believe me it wasn't my first choice, or my second or even my last choice. It was Lisa's birthday so I had to go, long story, I'll tell ya later but you're never gonna believe what happened. You are going to be so jealous.” I was so excited to tell him until I remembered the playoffs. I rambled on asking him questions faster than a batman car.

“So who won the play offs? Did he just award it to Nige or did Josh get to take my place? Please tell me Josh won. I couldn't stand it if Nigel won. Did you get to see it? How many people went to watch?”

“Whoa! Hang on. One question at a time,” Matthew said putting his hand up near my face. “No-one went to watch it, and no, I didn't get to see it, and no, Josh didn't win because no, he didn't take your place, and no, Nige didn't win either because you weren't here so Mr Higginbottom said we'd wait until this week when you got back and play the final then.” He gasped for breath as my jaw dropped open wide enough to let a whole army of flies swarm in. I was gob smacked.

"Yyy you mean," I stuttered, unable to get the words out, "I still get to play in the grand final. I'm still in?"

"Yep," said Matthew. "I volunteered to take your place but Mr H said that you won the heats and worked hard at school so you deserved to play it out."

"You're kidding right? You're pulling my leg."

"What? I'm not touching your leg, what are you talking about?" He looked at me confused. He's so dumb sometimes. "I'm not kidding; you get to play this Friday."

We arrived at our class room door. I don't think my jaw had returned to its proper position. It was still dragging along the ground flabbergasted. I looked inside and the coolest ever teacher was sitting at his desk in the coolest ever school in the whole world. I wanted to run up and give him a big hug but I thought that would be pretty uncool and I would embarrass myself if I did. I couldn't wait to tell him what happened.

Chapter 21: Good Things can Come out of Bad Things

t was probably the closest PlayStation game I had ever played but when I finally won the grand final, I made one of the weirdest, strangest decisions in my life. I decided to donate the winning game to the runner-up. That was Nigel, the nastiest boy in fifth grade. I had won five games *and* a console on the weekend so I decided it would be a nice idea to give somebody else some of my good luck.

And you know what; it actually felt really good to give something to some one. I'd never done that before except for birthdays and at Christmas time. It gave me a warm fuzzy feeling in my stomach when Nigel said "Gee thanks Ryan, that's way cool of you to give it to me after you won it," and he smiled. I'd never seen him smile before. He didn't look so mean. After that he even asked me if I wanted to be friends, which kinda scared me a bit.

Actually it was Mom's idea to give the prize to him, but when I thought about it, it was a pretty good suggestion. I guess Mom does know what she's talking about sometimes; well, probably all the time. She was definitely right when she said, "You know, sometimes good things *can* come out of bad things!"

THE END

I really hope you enjoyed this story and had a few laughs. I would love to hear what you thought about Ryan and the PS gang. Please leave me a review on Amazon or Goodreads so I know to write more about the PS Gang ☺☺.

In the meantime, it's time to read

Game On Boys 2 : Minecraft Madness
available now at Amazon as an eBook or print book, and look out for
Game On Boys 3 : No Girls Allowed coming soon

Made in the USA
Middletown, DE
18 December 2015